My "r" Sound Box®

WRITTEN BY JANE BELK MONCURE • ILLUSTRATED BY REBECCA THORNBURGH

The Child's World®
childsworld.com

Published by The Child's World®
1980 Lookout Drive • Mankato, MN 56003-1705
800-599-READ • www.childsworld.com

ISBN HARDCOVER: 9781503823211
ISBN PAPERBACK: 9781503831438
LCCN: 2017960383

Printed in the United States of America
PA02430

A NOTE TO PARENTS AND EDUCATORS:

Magic moon machines and five fat frogs are just a few of the fun things you can share with children by reading books with them. Reading aloud helps children in so many ways! It introduces them to new words, motivates them to develop their own reading skills, and expands their attention span and listening abilities. So it's important to find time each day to share a book or two . . . or three!

As you read with young children, you can help develop their understanding of how print works by talking about the parts of the book—the cover, the title, the illustrations, and the words that tell the story. As you read, use your finger to point to each word, modeling a gentle sweep from left to right.

Simple word games help develop important prereading skills, including an understanding of rhyme and alliteration (when words share the same beginning sound, such as "six" and "sand"). Try playing with words from a book you've just shared: "What other words start with the same sound as moon?" "Cat and hat, do those words rhyme?" The possibilities are endless—and so are the rewards!

My "r" Sound Box®

Little  had a box. "I will find things that begin with my **r** sound," he said.

"I will put them into my sound box."

Little  found rabbits and radishes. Did he put

the rabbits and the radishes into the box? He did.

Little  found a rooster. Did he put the rooster into the box with the rabbits and the radishes? He did.

Then he found a raccoon. The raccoon ran! Little

ran after the raccoon and put it into the box.

Then he saw a rat. The rat ran.

Little  ran after the rat and put it into the box. Then he ran down the road.

Soon, Little  met a reindeer.

The reindeer was too big for the  box, so Little found a rowboat.

He put the reindeer and the box with the
rat, the raccoon, the rooster, and the rabbits
into the rowboat.

There were no radishes left. The
rabbits had eaten the radishes.

Little  rowed down the river.

It started to rain. Little  put on his raincoat.

He rowed right into a rhinoceros!

The rhinoceros was too big for the rowboat.

So Little  found a raft.

He put all the animals on the raft.

He put the box on the raft, too.

But the raft ran into a rock! The reindeer, the rat, and the rooster fell off the raft.

Little  found a rope and rescued them.

"Now we will rest!" he said.

The rhinoceros, the rabbits, the raccoon, the reindeer, the rat, and the rooster rested under a rainbow.

Little  rested, too.

Then the rabbits said, "Let's run a race."

They ran up the road to a bush full of  roses. Little  picked roses for his box.

"Let's play 'Ring Around the Roses,'" he said.

And they did!

Little 's Word List

rabbit

raccoon

race

radish

raft

rain

rainbow

raincoat

rat

reindeer

rhinoceros

river

road

rock

rooster

rope

rose

rowboat

Other Words with Little

radio

ribbon

robot

raspberry

rice

rocket

rattle

ring

roof

razor

robe

rug

rectangle

robin

ruler

More to Do!

Little and his animal friends had a great time playing Ring Around the Roses. Here is another fun rhyming game for you to play!

Directions:

Make up your own verses using the same tune as "Ring Around the Roses." Use as many **r** words as you can think of. You'll also need to think of silly rhyming words. Here are some verses to get you started:

Rhyming:

Ring around the rabbit
Pocketful of babbit
Silly, silly,
We all fall down!
Ring around the rocket
Pocketful of zocket
Silly, silly,
We all fall down!

About the Author

Best-selling author Jane Belk Moncure (1926–2013) wrote more than 300 books throughout her teaching and writing career. After earning a master's degree in early childhood education from Columbia University, she became one of the pioneers in that field. In 1956, she helped form the Virginia Association for Early Childhood Education, which established the first statewide standards for teachers of young children.

Inspired by her work in the classroom, Mrs. Moncure's books became standards in primary education, and her name was recognized across the country. Her success was reflected not only in her books' popularity with parents, children, and educators, but also by numerous awards, including the 1984 C. S. Lewis Gold Medal Award.

About the Illustrator

Rebecca Thornburgh lives in a pleasantly spooky old house in Philadelphia. If she's not at her drawing table, she's reading—or singing with her band, called Reckless Amateurs. Rebecca has one husband, two daughters, and two silly dogs.